D1053491

Don't Kill Santa!

Don't Kill Santa!

Christmas Stories by Donald Davis

August House Publishers, Inc.
LITTLE ROCK

Copyright © 2006 by Donald Davis, Storyteller, Inc.
All rights reserved. This book, or parts thereof, may not be
reproduced or publicly performed in any form without permission.

Published 2006 by August House Publishers, Inc.
P.O. Box 3223, Little Rock, Arkansas 72203
501–372–5450
http://www.augusthouse.com

Printed in the United States of America

10 9 8 7 6 5 4 3 2 1

LIBRARY OF CONGRESS CATALOGING-IN-PUBLICATION DATA

Davis, Donald, 1944–
    Don't Kill Santa : holiday stories / by Donald Davis.
        p.   cm.
    ISBN-13: 978-0-87483-746-9 (alk. paper)
    ISBN-10: 0-87483-746-4 (alk. paper)
        1. Davis, Donald, 1944– —Homes and haunts—North Carolina.
    2. Authors, American—20th century—Biography. 3. Davis, Donald, 1944–
    —Childhood and youth. 4. North Carolina—Social life and customs.
    5. Davis, Donald, 1944– —Family. 6. Grandfathers—North Carolina.
    7. North Carolina—Biography. 8. Christmas—North Carolina. I. Title.
    PS3554.A93347Z463   2006
    813'.54—dc22
    [B]   2005048065

The paper used in this publication meets the minimum requirements of the
American National Standard for Information Sciences—Permanence of Paper
for Printed Library Materials, ANSI Z39.48–1984.

AUGUST HOUSE   PUBLISHERS   LITTLE ROCK

For Kathryn Tucker Windham,
whose love and friendship
are the best Christmas gifts ever

FOREWORD

There was a time when Santa Claus only came down the chimney. Since he had to carry everything in one sleigh, you could only ask for one toy.

It was a time when Santa Claus really did know everything no matter who you were or where you lived. And, it really did matter whether you were good or bad if you wanted to get anything from him for Christmas.

Back then Santa lived at the North Pole, was married to Mrs. Santa Claus, only wore red suits, had a huge team of elves, and crafted every single toy in the entire world.

That time does not have a date attached to it. No, the date is different for each one of us. It is a time usually called Childhood—yes, with a capital *C*.

These stories are visits to and memories of this Childhood at what was, for my family, the most magical time of the year: Christmas.

Magic always has two sides. Therefore, the stories and memories of Christmas are both happy and sad, funny and scary, light and dark. So it is with important times in our lives.

My only hope is that my memories will seed

yours, and, after visiting my childhood, your childhood of memories will be more alive and more appreciated—and that your stories will be told.

—DONALD DAVIS

CONTENTS

The Christmas
When It Snowed

WHEN MY BROTHER, JOE, AND I WERE little boys, the first stories that we loved were the stories that our daddy told us about "when he was a little boy." Each year during the Christmas season, we would be sure to ask him to tell us about "the Christmas when it snowed."

Of course there must have been more than one Christmas when it snowed during our father's childhood in the North Carolina mountains, but when we asked for the story, he always knew exactly what we meant, and the right story followed.

Our father was born in 1901 on a family farm far back in the Smoky Mountains. He used to tell us that it was a stretch to call it a farm since there was almost never enough of anything left over to sell. There were, eventually, ten surviving children of the thirteen born into the household, and simply feeding this household year-round was nearly an all-consuming task.

When the younger children started to school, their teacher was their oldest brother, Uncle Grover. He was born in 1885 and, before becoming a lawyer, taught eight of his younger brothers and sisters in a one-room school.

In 1910 Daddy was nine years old and in the fourth grade at the one-room school. It was two days before Christmas and the last day before school got out for the holidays. About the middle of the morning it started snowing.

The night before, Daddy had started coughing, and, as the snow day wore on, he was coughing more and more at school. Eventually he started having trouble breathing, and, after lunchtime at school, Uncle Grover decided it was time to send Daddy home early. By now it was really snowing and covering the ground.

It was about a mile-and-a-half walk from school back to their house. Uncle Grover decided to send Daddy's little sister, our Aunt Mary, to walk home with him. The two of them headed home in the snow.

As they walked, it snowed harder and harder, and Daddy had a harder and harder time breathing. He was coughing his head off and felt that he could barely get his breath.

Finally they got onto their own land but were still about a half-mile from home. Aunt Mary wasn't sure that Daddy could make it. She told him to wait while she ran home to get Granddaddy.

They were standing by a big log on the side of the road. Daddy and Mary raked the snow back from the leaves piled beside the log, Daddy lay down next to the log, and Mary covered him with leaves to keep him warm until she got back. Then she ran home.

As soon as she told their father what had happened, Granddaddy put on his coat and ran with her to find Daddy. By now the snow had completely covered the leaves with which she had covered him, and when they dug him out, he had fallen asleep in the leaves under the snow.

Granddaddy picked Daddy up and ran all the way home with him.

When they went in the door of the house, Grandmother was crying. "Oh Joe," she said. "It's not starting again, is it?" Granddaddy's first wife and three of their five children had died of whooping cough more than twenty years earlier, and when Grandmother heard Daddy's deep cough, it scared her to death.

They put Daddy to bed, wrapping him in quilts heated in the oven of the stove, and Granddaddy quickly saddled his horse to get the nearest doctor, who lived about three miles away.

When he returned home with Dr. France, who was actually a relative of the family, the doctor went into the room where Daddy was in the bed and began to examine him. He leaned over the bed and put his ear directly on Daddy's chest. He had him turn over and put his ear at different places on his back.

"Then," Daddy told us, "he got me to sit up and look out the window. While I was looking out of the window, the doctor pointed way out toward the barn and said, 'Little Joe, can you see something sitting on top of the barn in the snow?'"

Daddy told us that while he was straining to try to see through the falling snow, the doctor slapped him hard on the back. But the slap was just a distraction. It kept him from seeing that, just as he was slapped, the doctor had stuck a big, long needle under his ribs and right into one of his lungs.

Then the doctor pulled out of his lung what Daddy described to us as "a great big slug of bloody water," and as the water came out, he could breathe again!

After that ordeal, the doctor told my grandmother that Little Joe didn't have the whooping cough. No, he had what they thought sounded like "the new-monia" —and, the doctor told everyone, he was probably not going to die because he was "as strong as a little bull."

Dr. France told them to keep my daddy warm, feed him a lot of hot soup, and make him turn over every hour or so and beat him real hard on the back. In another day, Daddy was coughing a lot less and looking forward to the coming of Christmas in just two more days.

It kept slowly snowing through the coming day, and by Christmas Eve the entire world was covered with white. There really was going to be a white Christmas.

Before getting ready to go to bed on Christmas Eve, everyone did two things. First, each of the children picked out their best sock and, with a little tack, hung it along the edge of the mantle over the fireplace in the living room. They weren't sure about it, but they all hoped that maybe they had been good enough for Santa Claus to come by and leave something in the night.

The second thing they did before going to bed was to beg their father, my grandfather, to please tie up the dogs. "Tie up the dogs . . . please! Please tie up the dogs!" Every child entered into the plea.

"What for?" their father asked, with a laughing glint in his eye.

"The dogs will bark at the reindeer!" Uncle Harry explained. "The dogs will chase the reindeer . . . and Santa Claus will decide that it's not safe to land. He will pull up and go on by here and give whatever he has for us to somebody else!"

Finally, laughing all the while, Granddaddy went outside and tied the dogs up so they wouldn't chase the reindeer away. Now it was safe for everyone to go to bed.

Daddy told Joe-brother and me all about what happened next. He said that they were all in bed still trying to fall asleep when the dogs started barking like mad and there came a terrible screaming sound from somewhere beyond the barn.

All the children jumped up out of bed and ran into the kitchen, where they knew their mother and father were still up and about. When they got to the kitchen, their mother was helping their father on with his big coat as he then picked up his big shotgun and headed for the door.

"Don't shoot Santa Claus!" our daddy told us he himself cried out.

"I'm not going to shoot Santa Claus. That's not Santa Claus . . . something is in the pigs. It sounds like somebody is stealing one of our pigs on Christmas Eve!"

Then their mother spoke up. "Don't shoot a neighbor, Joe. If a neighbor has gotten so hungry that they are stealing a pig, don't shoot them on Christmas Eve!"

"I won't shoot a neighbor on Christmas Eve, Ella," Granddaddy answered her. "If it's a neighbor stealing the pig, I won't shoot them until next week! But I don't think it's a neighbor."

With that, he was out the door and into the snow with his gun in one hand and the kerosene lantern in the other.

In a few minutes everyone heard the gun fire, *Blam! Blam!* Then it was quiet. In no time Granddaddy came almost running back into the house.

"Put on your coats and hats," he said to everyone. "Even you, little Joe." He pointed to Daddy, who was out of the bed where he was supposed to be sick. "You wrap up in a blanket and I will carry you. There's something you've all got to see in case it rains and melts or the snow covers it up again . . . come on!"

Daddy wrapped up in a blanket. Then Granddaddy got him hugged up close under his big coat, which he actually buttoned over the both of them. Granddaddy got Daddy's little head up under his own chin where his full beard came down around Daddy's face and ears, keeping even that part of him warm, and they all started out through the snow and beyond the barn.

When they all got to the far side of the barn, they could see that part of the side of the pigpen had been

17

broken, but that it had also been temporarily and quickly fixed back. Then they could see, by the light of the lantern, that all over the snow there was blood . . . and bear tracks!

"Look!" Granddaddy pointed with the lantern. "Some old bear didn't eat enough before he went to bed for the winter. Looks like he woke up hungry in the night and decided to have one of our little pigs for his Christmas dinner! At least he knows who has the best pigs in Iron Duff!"

"Did you shoot him?" Uncle Harry asked.

"No," their daddy answered. "I just shot the gun a couple of times to be sure that he was scared on off. I followed up into the woods a little way to where it looked like he stopped and ate most of the pig. He took the rest with him."

Then the whole family made their way back to the house through the snow, and for the second time, they all went to bed in hopes that Santa Claus might actually come.

Daddy told us that he went to sleep dreaming of bears in the snow. The dogs didn't bark any more at all that night, and when everyone was awake the next day, they got up wondering whether Santa really had made a visit in the night. They were almost afraid to go to the fireplace to have a look.

When all of the children finally went into the living room, they couldn't believe their eyes. Even from across the room you could see that there was something in every single stocking hanging over the fireplace. As they jumped and cheered, Granddaddy said, "Why don't you see what you got?"

As they took down their stockings and began to feel inside, they made a great discovery. Every single child had gotten from Santa an orange of their very own, and every single child had an entire stick of candy that they could eat without having to share licks with anyone. Some got peppermint and some got horehound. And in the toe of each stocking, every child found a penny for each year old they were on that Christmas day.

"Santa Claus is rich!" Uncle Harry cried out. "Santa Claus is rich!"

The children all agreed. Santa Claus must be the richest man in the entire world! How could anyone be so wealthy as to be able to give every single child in the world their very own orange, their very own stick of candy, and know what kind of candy each of them would love the best? And who in the whole world could give every one of them a penny for every year they had lived? They simply could not take it all in.

Daddy told us that his stick of candy lasted for

nearly three weeks. Each day he would lick it three times: once to see if it was real, once to really taste it, and once to show that it was actually completely his. Then he would put it away and not lick it again until the next day.

As for the orange, he was simply planning to keep it forever and never eat it. He liked to rub the surface and smell the oil on his fingers.

Finally his mother told him that if he didn't eat the orange it would rot. He slowly spent three days eating it a piece at a time. But he saved the peel. It still had its good smell. He kept the peel on the table beside his bed, and every night before going to sleep he would rub it in his fingers, then sniff them as he fell asleep dreaming about someday getting to go to a place where oranges actually grew.

Later in the day, their mother fixed Christmas dinner for everyone. She fixed two chickens so everyone would have a whole piece of their own.

While they were eating, Grandmother said to Granddaddy, "Joe, I wish that we had known that the bear was going to get that little pig."

"Why, Ella?" he questioned.

"Because if we had known that the bear was going to get the pig, we could have taken that pig instead and we could have had it for our Christmas dinner!"

"No, Ella," he smiled. "We wouldn't want to have done that. You see, if we had eaten the pig, it would have fed us for one day. But, because the bear got the pig, we got a story out of it . . . and a story will feed us forever!"

And now, with every year that passes when the story is still told, now more than ninety years later, I am more sure that what Granddaddy said is and always will be true.

Jolly Old Saint Nicholas

DADDY'S STORY ABOUT THE CHRISTMAS when it snowed was a true story from his family and his own life. There were, however, other stories Joe-brother and I heard in our storytelling family that were not as true.

Uncle Frank was the family storytelling champion. He turned every event that happened—and many did—into a huge story. All through my growing-up years I could listen to my Uncle Frank tell stories for hours and never grow tired of them.

When we would go to visit Uncle Frank (he now lived in the house in which my father had grown up, the very house from which they had heard the little pig screaming), his near neighbor Silas Jolly would often be there. Silas was usually called "the *real* storyteller," and he and Uncle Frank could sit on the porch or in the yard for hours swapping tales that continued to grow in exaggeration the longer we listened.

Both Silas and Uncle Frank had created families of imaginary relatives for one another. Through the years they gradually created dozens of stories about the foolishness of one another's imaginary kin. It was marvelous.

One of these often-retold stories happened at Christmas. Both Silas and Uncle Frank swore it to be "true whether it happened or not"! The story involved one of Silas's imaginary cousins whom he and Uncle Frank called "Tracker." (They both told us that the fact that no one had ever met Tracker had nothing to do with the fact that he did not exist.)

We were told that Tracker got his name because he was born with a remarkable talent that his family noticed before he was old enough to walk: he had a reputation even as a crawler for his photographic memory for the ground (Silas called it a "topographic mind").

This meant that he simply never got lost. He could remember the most minute detail of the ground beneath his feet, right down to particular blades of grass and grains of sand. It was this remarkable ability that had gained him his name before he could walk.

Tracker was most unusual. Uncle Frank told us that when he was taken to ride in the car, Tracker would ride with the window rolled down and his head hanging out the window so he could watch the road passing by underneath in order to tell, from his topographic memory of the ground, where they had been and where they were going.

Silas then told us that it was no fun having him along for a ride in the wintertime. Tracker insisted on sticking his head out the window, and so he froze everyone else in the car half to death. (This assertion was more mysterious to us as children since we also remembered occasions on which Silas told us that he himself had never ridden in a car in his life.)

At each holiday season a great portion of the family gathered at Uncle Frank's house because this was, after all, the home place of the Iron Duff Davises. Over the years all the small out-of-town cousins were visited by Santa Claus while they were at Uncle Frank's house for Christmas. They never saw him, of course, but no matter how far from home they were, St. Nicholas always brought their presents.

One year, Uncle Frank got an idea. "Why don't I make arrangements," he said to himself, "to have old Santa Claus himself show up and deliver the presents on Christmas morning?"

When he shared his plan with his neighbor, Silas wanted to know just how he was going to manage that.

"It's simple," Uncle Frank answered. "They've

got a Santa Claus suit up at Belk's Department Store. I'm going to borrow it over Christmas and dress up for the little ones."

"Aw, Frank," Silas objected, "they'll know it's you, and that won't be any fun!"

Uncle Frank knew that was probably true, but he didn't want to give up on the idea.

Silas suggested the idea first and Uncle Frank liked the suggestion, so he decided to hire Tracker Jolly to wear the Santa Claus suit and bring presents to all the little Davis children on Christmas morning.

And so the plan was made. Uncle Frank borrowed the Santa Claus suit from Belk's a few days before Christmas and took it, along with all the cousins', nieces', and nephews' presents, to the Jollys' house. The project was now in Tracker's hands.

Christmas Eve arrived. Tracker was excited. He loaded all the presents in the big sack early in the afternoon, even though he wasn't to appear at Uncle Frank's house until breakfasttime the next morning. He put on the Santa Claus costume and took it off a half-dozen times.

His only concern was the weight of the sack of toys. With all those children at Uncle Frank's for Christmas, Tracker was carrying an extra heavy load.

"I've got an idea!" he told Silas. "Why don't I take

all the toys down to Mr. Davis's barn and take the suit there, too? I can make two or three loads if they are too heavy. Then I'll spend the night at the barn, and in the morning I'll put the suit on there and be real close to the house for one stout haul. The best I can remember it's only a hundred and forty-six rocks, three cowpies, six thousand and thirty blades of dead grass, three rotten planks and eleven thousand and one grains of sand from the barn to the house!"

"Why, that's a real good idea," Silas agreed.

Tracker, aided by Silas and Uncle Frank, made several trips to the barn before dark to get everything set up for his performance as Santa Claus. Tracker slept on the hay in the barn, dreaming of what a nice Christmas this would be. The next morning, he got up, put on the Santa Claus suit, put all the toys in one big sack, slung it over his shoulder, and opened the barn door to get on with his mission.

To his horror, the world looked like a Christmas card. The ground was completely covered with a soft blanket of snow, and Tracker—unable to see the ground—had no idea which way to go to get to Uncle Frank's house.

He would have been able to see the house if he had only looked up, but since he had never done such a thing in his life, he couldn't really be expected to start now—especially not with that heavy load of toys on his back.

For a few moments he panicked. *I'm lost! I'm lost!* he thought. Then he thought to look at the floor back inside the barn door and remembered that he was starting out in the barn.

Finally Tracker made a decision. He would wander, directionless, out into the snow in hopes that he would either see something sticking up from the ground that would help him or meet someone who could direct him to Uncle Frank's house. He did try kicking the snow aside for a few steps, but even he could see that would take so long Christmas would be gone before he got out of the barnyard.

And so Tracker started out on his frustrating journey across the unknown land of snow. He wandered right past Uncle Frank's house, right through the yard, but since he didn't look up and since he couldn't see the ground, he didn't know where he was.

He wandered across the bottom field and right up through the Jolly Cove quite near his own home, but he still didn't know where he was. He wandered in a big circle around the fish pond and back toward Uncle Frank's barn where he had gotten lost to begin with.

Tracker began to despair. *There's nobody out here. Everybody's staying in the house and waiting for me, and*

I don't know how to get there unless one of them comes out to help, and nobody's coming.

Then, miraculously, he came upon a set of tracks in the snow. "Oh! Oh!" Tracker shouted. "I am saved! I am found! I will just follow these tracks until I catch up with whoever I'm following, and I know it will be someone who will help me get to Mr. Davis's house."

With new resolve, Tracker began following, in hearty pursuit of help, his own tracks!

For the second time, he passed through Uncle Frank's yard. For the second time, he crossed the bottom and trudged up into the cove. For the second time, he passed his own house, and for the second time, as he turned back toward the barn, he began to despair.

Whoever I'm following is a-walking too fast. I can't catch him, not with this big load I'm a-carrying! He was about ready to give up.

And then, suddenly, there were *two* sets of tracks!

"Oh, look!" Tracker exclaimed to himself. "Two of them! I'm a-following two of them." He sped up his pace, figuring that with two people to follow he had twice as many chances to get help.

This new burst of hope drove him on so that it seemed like no time until he was following three people, and then it was four!

Around and around he traipsed, as Christmas

morning came and went, following his own round-and-round tracks. He was sure he was finally on the main road to somewhere because everybody seemed to be going the same way.

No one knows how long this might have gone on had not, by great good fortune, the sun come out in the afternoon and begun to melt the snow. At last Tracker came to a place where the snow was gone and he could see the ground. He saw that he was right in Uncle Frank's front yard, and kicking the last few feet of snow aside, he found his way to the steps and approached the front door of the house.

Uncle Frank was exhausted. All day long he had been promising the children that Santa Claus was coming, and he was fast running out of excuses about why he had not yet arrived. It was a time of real comfort and joy when a knock came and Uncle Frank opened the door to see Tracker—who had probably walked close to twenty miles by now, carrying that sack of presents every step of the way.

"Look, children!" Uncle Frank almost wept. "I told you he was coming! It's Jolly old Saint Nicholas!" The day was saved.

Uncle Frank was afraid to ask Tracker what had happened; he wasn't sure he was up to hearing the explanation. He did get a clue when Tracker asked him later in the day, "Mr. Davis, did about fifteen or twenty people come by here a little while ago?"

When Uncle Frank said no, Tracker concluded the matter. "Then I'm glad I quit following them when I did, or there's no telling where I might have ended up!"

And as for all Uncle Frank's little nieces and nephews? The ones that were there were all happy for Santa Claus to go back to delivering presents in the night the way he always had. And the ones that weren't there were glad the whole thing had happened. For from then on they got to hear, ever year, the story of how Tracker followed himself all the way to Uncle Frank's house—whether it ever really happened or not!

Christmas in Sulpher Springs

MOST OF OUR ACQUAINTANCE WITH Christmas on our father's side of the family actually came through stories of his childhood. Daddy did not marry until he was in his mid-forties. Most of his sisters and brothers were even older. We were far removed from the actual time of their childhood . . . but not the stories.

Joe-brother and I were among the last and youngest of the Davis cousins. The others were older and already building their own at-home traditions. Daddy's outlying family came for visits mostly in the summertime, not the Christmas holidays.

It was Mother's side of the family with whom we actually spent our early years at Christmas. This being our only experience of Christmas, our assumption was that the whole world celebrated the holiday as we did. Only much later did we realize the gift of wonder we received through these family childhood Christmas customs.

Christmas in Sulpher Springs was a strangely fascinating combination of two worlds, old and new. Traditional mountain customs and ancient observations formed the heart and soul of the season. At the same time, the new power of advertising and the proliferation of newspapers and radios had made us part of the "modern" world of commercialized holidays.

Generations-old gift-making traditions still lived on all over Nantahala County. But many homemade crafts had to come to town to be sold side-by-side with the MADE IN JAPAN junk toys so highly prized by children of all ages. Winning and losing took place even at Christmas and even in that idyllic world.

Our mother's family began to gather as soon as school was out. Sulpher Springs was still "home" to more than a dozen aunts and uncles who had left the mountains to seek their fortunes from Chicago to Florida, but who always planned to come home . . . some day.

Christmas, like summertime, was a brief season of homecoming. The whole extended matriarchal family came pouring in, with more and more new little cousins each year—tumbling from cars with strange license tags—to push us from our own beds for two weeks and eat everything Mother had put up at the cannery the summer before.

It was a wonderful time of holiday smells and special food, of staying up late and listening to the old people talk. It was a time for telling stories and feeling the world was in its proper place.

On Christmas mornings we loaded up in the blue Dodge and went to Grandmother's house. Grandmother and Granddaddy lived nearly twenty miles out of Sulpher Springs up on Cedar Fork Mountain. It took almost an hour to get there on the curving roads out through Bowlegged Valley and past Crabtree Creek, even though an eight-foot-wide strip of road was paved nearly all the way to their house.

It was an excellent ride. In early years Mother had not learned to drive, and Daddy took advantage of that fact by driving fast enough to scare her all the way. Joe-brother and I played in the floor of the back seat, trying to get away from Daddy's ever-present cigar smoke, which was much worse in winter when the windows were rolled up and the heater was turned on.

The last part of the drive was a two-mile climb up and over the gap in Cedar Fork Mountain. Daddy had a special little game he played with himself (and with the Dodge) on this part of the trip. The game was to see how far up Cedar Fork he could get before he had to shift the Dodge down into second gear.

As soon as we passed the sawmill below Crabtree Creek, it was time for the game to begin. From here, the road ran straight up and over Sutton Farm Hill, then down through a long dip and right up the mountain toward Cedar Fork Gap.

Daddy poured on the gas and puffed the cigar at the same time. Mother always protested, but weakly. "Don't go too fast," she would say, which always made him stick the accelerator right to the floor.

We topped Sutton Farm Hill at forty-five miles an hour and started down the last dip before climbing the big mountain. Daddy kept it on the floor. Joe-brother and I peeked over the seat so that we could see the speedometer. The needle climbed to fifty . . . fifty-five . . .

If you should meet another car on the narrow strip of pavement, you had to each put two wheels off in the gravel to pass safely. At this speed, that would have been totally out of the question. But here the road was straight, and Daddy could see that nothing was coming.

"Please slow down!" Mother pleaded.

Now we were pulling up the mountain, and even with the gas pedal on the floor, the Dodge was slowing down. Up, up, up the steep hill we went. Joe-brother and I could see the speedometer needle dropping. Fifty . . . forty-five . . . forty . . . thirty-five . . .

It was coming—the time we were waiting for. Up ahead was "Second Gear Curve." That's where it always happened: the Dodge went into second gear, and more importantly, Daddy gave his interpretation of the event for the day. Joe-brother and I were ready for it.

As the Dodge approached "Second Gear Curve," the speedometer dropped to thirty, then twenty-five. We entered the curve. It was time.

Daddy bit down on the cigar, pushed in the clutch, and threw the gearshift of the Dodge into second gear. At the same time he grinned, looked at Mother, and this time said, "This six-cylinder Dodge wouldn't pull a wet booger out of a baby's nose . . . with the baby blowing to boot!"

Mother only turned a little bit red this time. Some of his worst interpretations in the past had included terms like "greasy strings" and "tomcat's rear ends." A baby's booger wasn't very bad at all.

By the time all the blush had left Mother's face, we were over the top of Cedar Fork and almost to Grandmother's house.

There was a mile-long unpaved farm road that

.ed through the woods to our grandmother's house, but we seldom drove down it to the house, especially in wintertime. Granddaddy was of that suspicious breed who regarded having company as something between a bother and an outright danger. To be sure that no wandering tourist accidently drove down the road to his house, he simply refused to maintain it, so that he not only allowed it to erode but even dug it out at times and encouraged it to wash. Only *he* knew exactly how you had to drive at any given time to keep your wheels on the high spots, avoid the rocks, and keep from cracking an oil pan—or worse. The road served better than a mine field as a deterrent to unwanted company.

Sometimes we tried the road in the summer when the weather was dry. But now, as on most occasions, we drove on down the highway parallel to the unpaved road until we were through the woods and below Grandmother's house near the mailbox.

There, Daddy pulled the Dodge off onto the grassy side of the road where it would soon be joined by the cars of aunts, uncles, and loads of cousins. We opened the trunk, decided who would carry which bundles of goods and presents, and walked through a stand of hemlocks up the worn trail from the mailbox to the house.

"I hope Granddaddy sees that it's relatives before he starts shooting at us," cousin George would always joke.

His mother would reassure him. "Grandmother unloads all his guns on Christmas Day."

Finally, at the house, we entered another world.

Grandmother and Granddaddy lived in a big, two-story T-shaped log house. It was two rooms wide in the front—a living room and a bedroom—with a hall running back through the middle. The kitchen was the one room on the back and had been added on to the log house some years after it was originally built. It even had a root cellar dug beneath it for potatoes, turnips, carrots, and the like.

The upstairs of the house, reached by small, narrow stairs from the hall beside the kitchen, was really a huge two-part bedroom, with a variety of straw-tick and feather-mattress beds. Mother and her five brothers and six sisters had all been born in that house and had all slept upstairs while Grandmother and Granddaddy slept down in the big front bedroom, as they still did to this very day.

The house had no electricity and no running water. There were kerosene lamps everywhere and a few brilliant Aladdin gas lamps in the main living areas. Water was carried in from a spring about a hundred feet around the slope of the hill from the kitchen door.

The log house was always warm. There was a big wood cookstove in the kitchen. It held a reservoir of water, which the fire heated. In the living room stood a big Warm Morning wood heater. It had adjustable chrome-plated drafts on the front that no one but Granddaddy was allowed to open or close.

The first job of the day was to find a Christmas tree. Granddaddy, tempered as he was, never took care of this task ahead of time. We were instructed by Grandmother to "get a big one—not a floppy cedar tree like all the neighbors get, but a white pine tree with good, strong limbs."

There was a particular reason that a white pine tree was in order rather than a cedar tree. The reason was to be found in a wooden box of unknown origin that Grandmother kept hidden in the back recesses of the wardrobe in her bedroom. The box contained her only Christmas tree decorations: a set of twenty-three wooden candleholders—had there once been an even two dozen?—mounted on clips like short clothespins. These could be clipped to the Christmas tree . . . if the limbs were strong and well spaced.

The candleholders were varnished, unpainted natural wood. No one knew where they came from, whether they were homemade or bought. Grandmother had simply inherited them from her mother. The reason for the white pine was clear: a cedar, with its limber branches and close-spaced foliage, would never work. The limbs wouldn't support the weight, and the candles would set the tree on fire. White pine was perfect. It had stiff, strong limbs, spaced far enough apart and graduated so that the candles were stable and safe.

Each year Mother would bring twenty-three fresh white candles to go on the tree. While we were tramping after Daddy and the uncles in search of the proper tree, Mother and the aunts would clean the candleholders of wax residue and fit the new candles into the holders.

As soon as we found a tree everyone agreed on (it never took very long), one of the uncles would cut it down with a handsaw, flush with the ground, after which we would drag it back to the house and another uncle would nail crossed pieces of plank to the bottom to make it stand up.

Now it was time to decorate. The adults clipped on the candleholders. Each person got to pin one on the tree, after which they fussed like children over who got to put on the extras. Everyone had a different memory as to "who did it last year."

While this was going on, Grandmother was in the kitchen with the children. She would get out an eggbeater, a big crockery mixing bowl, and a box of Ivory Snow flakes bought especially for this occasion. We would put a tiny bit of water into the mixing bowl, add some Ivory Snow flakes, and watch her beat it into mountains of whipped "snow." Then we children would frost the white pine tree with several bowls of this bubbly snow, which, when it dried, actually looked like a frosting of dry, midwinter snowflakes.

The finished tree was all green and white. The grownups would light the candles, under Grandmother's direction, a few minutes at a time, then blow them out for fear that, unwatched, they would set the tree (and that meant the whole log house!) on fire. Even Granddaddy had to "allow as how it was a purty tree."

We would finally eat Christmas dinner about two o'clock in the afternoon, and some time after that, return home to take up what Santa Claus had brought, which gifts we had briefly checked out and left behind earlier in order to go to Grandmother's house.

In later years, after Granddaddy died and Grandmother moved in with her sister, things seemed to fall apart. Sometimes everyone would come to our house, but for most of the time, the growing cousins wanted to stay at home for Christmas and the number of out-of-state cars in the driveway seemed to get smaller each year.

Gradually, Joe-brother and I also preferred to stay at our own house on Christmas. Santa Claus seemed to bring us bigger toys as we got older. What we wanted to do was spend the day with our own new stuff and maybe see Grandmother later.

Our tree at home got bigger and more decorated. Grandmother now had no tree at all.

The Year
We Lost Our Presents

ONE CHRISTMAS JOE-BROTHER AND I LOST
our presents. Joe-brother was six years old and I was
eight.

Very often, both of us wanted the same things for
Christmas, and this was one of those years. The
newest toy—which all the kids we knew wanted—
was Lincoln Logs. Some of our friends already had
them, and we were fascinated by the notched-end
building logs in various lengths and the green-slat
roof-pieces with which whole farmsteads of houses,
barns, and fences could be built. The logs were especially fascinating in that there were still a lot of log
houses in Nantahala County at the time, and we had
a lot of full-sized models we wanted to duplicate.

Joe-brother and I thought that with two sets of
the logs we would have enough to build anything we

could think of, so we each asked Santa Claus for the biggest possible set of Lincoln Logs.

On Christmas morning, our wishes came true. There, under the Christmas tree, were two big sets of dark brown Lincoln Logs. We built a three-story house and a big barn and still had enough logs left to build a fence around both of them to boot.

Daddy always got a lot of Christmas gifts from salesmen who called on him at the hardware store. Since he was a known tobacco chewer and cigar smoker, a lot of his Christmas gifts consisted of plugs of Penn's Natural Leaf Chewing Tobacco and Tampa Nugget Cigars—favorites of his.

This year was no exception. He came home with enough tobacco and cigars to last through the coming year, and over Mother's objections, he put all of them in the refrigerator, "where they will stay nice and fresh," he said.

One gift this year was, however, different. In the midst of all the Tampa Nugget boxes was a strange cigar box. Someone who had not known about Daddy's brand preferences had given him a big box of long, almost black, Marsh Wheeling Cigars. The mouth end of the long cigars ended in a twist of tobacco that had to be either clipped or broken off before air would come through and the cigar could be smoked.

Daddy smoked one of these monsters about halfway through. Mother coughed and complained with every breath of smoke he exhaled.

"Those cigars," he finally declared, "will take the hair off your tonsils." He ground the cigar out in his ashtray, then closed the box and put the remainder in his underwear drawer instead of the refrigerator.

"Maybe I'll give them to Brown Hill next time he comes to tear down birds' nests."

Later in the day, as he watched us building with the Lincoln Logs, it occurred to him that the big cigars looked a lot like our Lincoln Logs (which were, he declared, probably easier to smoke). He suggested that we just add the cigars to the Lincoln Log sets and use them for building zigzag rail fences and such. We gladly accepted the gift, and the cigar logs worked very well.

After Christmas dinner, we returned to the Lincoln Logs and built a whole mountain farmstead of buildings, complete with a little pigpen built out of cigar logs.

By midafternoon the dinnertime relatives had left, all the dishes were washed, and Daddy had settled in his chair to sleep and snore for a while. Joe-brother and I were beginning to get tired of our initial building projects. We needed some excitement.

Finally I said, "Would you like to learn how to smoke one of these cigars?"

"Do you know how?" Joe-brother asked.

"I can show you how," I answered, with as such self-assurance as possible. "We'd better just take one of them, so Daddy won't notice in case he counts them."

We went through the kitchen, where I picked up a handful of "strike anywhere" matches from the shelf above the woodstove. We slipped out the back door and across the yard toward the garage.

The garage was a wooden building with a peaked roof. It was just big enough to hold one car and a few storage shelves in the back. There was a woodshed built onto the rear of the garage, and it had an almost-flat tin roof that butted against the garage just below the end gable. Since the woodshed was behind the garage, and its flat tin roof was hidden from the house by the peak of the garage, it made a good hideout. I had used it often.

We climbed the wooden fence that ran to the corner of the woodshed, then swung up onto the tin roof, out of sight of anyone who might be watching from the house. It never occurred to me that anyone might see the smoke rising from our hiding place, but as it happened, no one did.

There we unwrapped the cellophane from the big

cigar. "I'll do the hard part," I said, taking the cigar and breaking off the twisted tip, then opening a bigger hole in the end with the stick-end of the wooden match. I tried to do this just as I had seen Daddy do it on the one he had smoked. The hole I made looked plenty big for the air to come through.

"What do I do?" Joe-brother asked with innocent eagerness.

"Just put the cigar in your mouth," I instructed. Joe-brother did as he was told. "When I light the match and hold it up to the cigar, take a big, deep breath, then blow it out. Suck in, take the cigar out of your mouth, and blow out. Just do that over and over again, and you're smoking! But . . . don't dare stop and let it go out. Keep it going!"

I struck the match, and Joe-brother did exactly as I had told him. For the next twenty minutes, every breath of air he drew came into his lungs through the now-diminishing black cigar. As the cigar burned down, all the color began to drain out of Joe-brother. It was replaced by a strange, unnatural color—a green not at all like the healthy green of Christmas, but one with a pale yellowish tint.

About the time the cigar burned down to where Joe-brother couldn't hold it anymore, he slumped down against the end of the garage and dropped the cigar butt. It rolled down the slope of the tin roof and disappeared off the edge and out of sight.

Just then the back door of the house opened, and Mother called us to come to supper. I took one look at Joe-brother and decided it was time for me to abandon him right then and there.

When I got to the back door, Mother was waiting and holding it open as she looked for us. "Come in," she said. "Where's Joe-brother?"

I shrugged my shoulders in an I-don't-know kind of shrug, passed her by, and never said a word.

We both saw Joe-brother at the same time. He was running as fast as he could across the back yard toward us. I couldn't figure out how he had gotten off the roof so quickly, unless he had flopped over and rolled off the slope the same way the cigar butt had.

As he ran, he was vomiting—fast and hard. I thought that it was a good thing Mother was calling us to supper, because he was going to need food. He was losing everything he had had to eat since way before Christmas.

Our house had been built without a bathroom, but in more recent years a part of the back porch had been enclosed to make one. When Joe-brother got to the door, Mother grabbed him by the back of his overalls and hoisted him straight from the porch up into the bathroom. Once there, she dropped him, slimy clothes and all, straight into the big claw-footed bathtub.

On one of our trips to town, Mother had bought a hair-washing contraption at Jones's Drug Store. It was a rubber hose with a fitting you could push on over the tub faucet and a sprayer at the other end to create a nice hair-rinsing spray. Mother pushed the fitting onto the faucet and turned the water on full force. She quickly adjusted the temperature, and then she sprayed Joe-brother—face, clothes, and all—over and over again, every time he was sick.

I did hope that Joe-brother would live, but I was not at all looking forward to his recovering enough to explain what had happened there behind the garage. Finally he fell over in the bottom of the big bathtub like a limp washed-out rag, and the vomiting was over.

From the smell of things, Mother seemed to know what had happened before Joe-brother even began to tell her about it. Still, she asked, and Joe-brother told her every single detail of the story. She didn't look at him; instead, she stared at me with fire in her eyes while she listened.

When Joe-brother was finished, Mother said, "Go get a switch."

I did—a good one, to keep her from sending me back if it didn't pass her inspection. She wore it out on my legs. I now knew Joe-brother would live, because the grin on his face got bigger and bigger with every blow of the switch. Soon he was laughing his head off.

Later in the day, when we looked for them to play with, the Lincoln Logs had disappeared. Joe-brother asked Daddy where they were. "They've been repossessed," was his answer. Neither of us knew what that meant.

The Lincoln Logs reappeared sometime after the Fourth of July, but we never did see the Marsh Wheeling Cigars again.

The Myrrh

IT WAS THE YEAR AFTER WE GOT THE
Lincoln Logs that I was in my first Christmas play at
church.

The Methodist church in Sulpher Springs was a
brick building right in the middle of town on "Old
Main Street" at the corner of Oak. It faced Main
straight across from the post office, and right across
Oak Street to the side was the hardware store.

The main part of the church building was the
sanctuary, built a half-story above ground level so that
a wide set of ten steps led up to the door. You were
supposed to go up steps, I assumed, to go to church.

Under the sanctuary was a basement, only half-
underground, with Sunday school rooms for adults.
There was also a kitchen and a big room the adults
called the "fellowship hall." On the back side of the
church was the "new Sunday school building," with
two floors of classrooms, mostly for children.

This was the "town church," as opposed to the many white frame "country churches"—some Methodist, more Baptist (of every possible variety)—that centered every community and marked most crossroads in Nantahala County.

Our church was constructed of dark red brick and had a dome on the top instead of a steeple. It had an organ and stained glass windows with pictures of Jesus, angels, and Moses on them. Under each of these windows were the names of dead people whose families had paid for the windows. At least, that's what Hayden Campbell told Joe-brother.

Inside the front door, in what Daddy called the "vestibule," near where the coatrack and hatracks were, was a sign board with the names of all those who were in "Our Country's Service." There were gold stars beside some of the names, and Daddy told us those were the men who had been killed in the war.

Mrs. Minnie Yarborough was in charge of the Children's Department. Mrs. Minnie's husband, Mr. Leonard Yarborough, ran the Esso station, another block on down Oak Street at the corner of Railroad Street. (The Esso station was not an Old Main Street business.) He also taught the Old Men's Regular Bible Class in Sunday School.

On the Sunday after Thanksgiving, Mrs. Minnie

came into Sunday school and asked: "Now, who would like to be in this year's Christmas play? It will be at six o'clock on Christmas Eve and will be over in plenty of time before Santa Claus comes."

Joe-brother and I both raised our hands, and that very afternoon at four o'clock Daddy took us back to the church to start Christmas play practice.

Mrs. Minnie explained the play. We were going to act out her version of the Christmas story.

A big manger-scene set was being built by Mr. Yarborough. It would go right where the pulpit in the church was. Mary and Joseph and the baby Jesus would be in the manger scene from the start. Then all of the people and animals who came to visit the baby Jesus would come in, one at a time, singing their own special Christmas songs.

At the very end, Santa Claus would arrive and give everybody candy—even the baby Jesus, we guessed.

She went through the parts and had us hold up our hands to show which parts we would like to have. Everybody held up their hands for all of the parts, so Mrs. Minnie was the one who had to decide.

"Joey and Laura Ray Smith will be Mary and Joseph. They're the tallest," said Mrs. Minnie while we giggled for some unknown reason about Mary and

Joseph being played by a brother and sister. (We could all see that they didn't like the idea very much either.)

"Who gets to be the baby Jesus?" we all asked.

"The baby Jesus," Mrs. Minnie explained, "will be symbolized by a flashlight shining out of the top of the manger." None of us got the symbolism, but nobody said anything; maybe we just weren't old enough to understand.

Finally Mrs. Minnie got down to Joe-brother and me. Joe-brother was to be a shepherd, and I was to be one of the Wise Men.

For the next two Sunday afternoons we practiced, with Mrs. Minnie playing the piano while we sang. Joe-brother and the other shepherds had it hard. They had to sing a song called "While Shepherds Watched Their Flocks by Night," a song we had never heard of, so they had to learn it from the start.

The three of us Wise Men were much luckier. We were to sing "We Three Kings," and I already knew that. It was going to be wonderful. We Three Kings —Red McElroy, Freddie Patton, and I—would come down the aisle singing the first verse together. Then we would turn around, face the congregation, and each sing his own solo verse in front of the entire church. I was the third and last Wise Man. My gift was myrrh, and I would sing my verse about it before presenting it at the manger of the baby Jesus.

We were each responsible for our own costumes.

On the Saturday before Christmas Eve, Mother and Daddy helped Joe-brother and me get our costumes together. I had already picked out Daddy's blue-striped bathrobe for myself, but Joe-brother got to it first. Mother said to let him keep it, because Wise Men could "do better than that."

She put the bathrobe on Joe-brother, turned it under, and pinned it up at the bottom so it would be short enough for him. His headgear was a towel pulled tightly over his head, with a necktie tied as a headband around his forehead so the excess towel hung down his back. . He looked like an Arab in the comic strips.

As for me, being a wealthy Wise Man, Mother had another idea. I got to wear her good nylon robe. It felt like silk to me, with a paisley print mostly in reds and purples. What could be finer? It came to below my knees but not all the way to the floor, so it didn't need to be pinned up. My turban was made from a dark red silk scarf wrapped around my head with a costume-jeweled pin of Mother's holding it together on my forehead.

Joe-brother and I both looked wonderful.

Daddy had helped us with our props. He had thought ahead of time and taken a limber maple limb, soaked it in hot water in the bathtub, and gradually bent and tied the end into a shepherd's crook for Joe-brother. Now it was dry and stiff. He untied the string and it looked perfect.

The only thing I needed was the myrrh.

There was not a lot of myrrh to be found in Sulpher Springs, and Mother and Daddy had quite a time just figuring out what it was, anyway. Finally Daddy disappeared. He came back in the room with a pretty glass bottle he had taken from the cedar chest.

Mother said, "He can't take that to church. That's a whiskey decanter. You can't let him use that!" Daddy just laughed and said of course we could.

None of us could figure out what myrrh ought to look like in the bottle. My verse of the song called it a "bitter perfume." We finally decided to fill the bottle with coffee, as everyone agreed that a bright color wouldn't look very bitter.

Now we were ready, except for the shoes. Mother dug in the closet and brought out our summertime sandals. We would have to carry them to church in a paper bag because it was so cold. We would wear our regular shoes and socks on the way but change into the sandals before the play started.

We were ready.

On Christmas Eve we all went to the church at four o'clock in the afternoon. Mrs. Minnie was waiting for us. We put on our costumes for a "dress rehearsal." Everything went very well. We were all excited and ready for the real show.

While we were down in the church basement waiting for the people to come in and watching the clock inch toward six o'clock, Mrs. Minnie called me over to the side.

"Honey"—she called everybody "Honey"—"you sure do look nice, but your pants are showing between your robe and your sandals. Now you just slip off your pants so you'll look more like you're supposed to. The real Wise Men didn't have any pants."

I didn't like that idea, but I did what Mrs. Minnie told me to do. After all, she was the director. Once my blue jeans were safely in the paper sack with my shoes and socks, Mrs. Minnie retied the knot in the sash around the robe's waist that Mother had so carefully knotted before we had left home.

At last it was six o'clock—time for the big show to begin. The church bell rang. The organist began to play "O Come, All Ye Faithful," and Mrs. Minnie herded all of us up and into the vestibule so that we could begin.

Mary and Joseph came in while the rest of us, from the back, sang "Gentle Mary Laid Her Child." Laura Ray knelt at the end of the manger, not so much out of reverence as so she could switch on the flashlight that stood for the baby Jesus.

Next all the angels came in singing. Their song was "Hark! The Herald Angels Sing." Some of the smallest angels wandered all over the church, forgetting the words and finally hollering "Mama!" until they were at last herded in the right direction and lined up in the front.

Next came the shepherds. They had finally learned their song, and so they proudly sang "While Shepherds Watched Their Flocks by Night." Some carried crooks, and others carried stuffed animals of several varieties, all covered with drugstore cotton to make them look like sheep.

Now it was our turn.

"We three kings of orient are . . ." In practice, Red McElroy had always sung the next line as "trying to smoke a loaded cigar . . . *Bang!*" Even tonight, we all had the giggles until we got past that part. We kept singing.

" . . . bearing gifts we traverse afar; field and fountain, moor and mountain; following yonder star . . ." By now the three of us had sung our way side-by-side clear down the church aisle. Now we turned around, faced the congregation, and got ready for our solo verses.

Red McElroy was first. He sang *"Born a king on Bethlehem's plain . . ."* and presented the baby flashlight with a big, gold-painted brick.

Freddie Patton was next. He sang about frankincense, put a perfume bottle full of green colored water beside the manger, and bowed deeply to the congregation. There was a bit of laughter following his deep bow.

Now it was really my turn.

As I stepped to the center, I sensed a giggle run through the congregation. I thought that they had not yet settled down from Freddie's bow. The music was playing, so I had to start singing: *"Myrrh is mine, its bitter perfume . . ."* I held up the whiskey decanter filled with coffee. Some of the big kids on the front row actually laughed out loud. *". . . breathes a life of gathering gloom."* The laughter grew and so I put on my loudest and most dramatic voice: *". . . sorrowing, sighing, bleeding, dying . . ."* They were actually pointing at me now as they laughed out loud, and I sang at the top of my voice, *". . . sealed in a stone-cold tomb."*

Suddenly I became aware of where everyone was pointing. I looked down. Then and there I saw that the knot Mrs. Minnie had retied in my sash had come loose, and that there I stood, in front of the entire congregation, in the *spotlights,* singing at the top of my voice, with Mother's nylon robe hanging completely open in front. I had no pants on.

Those final words—*sealed in a stone-cold tomb*—seemed to ring through the air, and I dropped the myrrh.

Red and Freddie sang *"Star of wonder, star of light..."* just like nothing had happened, and the congregation laughed as I ran out of the sanctuary with the robe streaming out behind me.

The next year the adult choir sang on Christmas Eve, and no one ever mentioned what had happened the year before. For many years, there was a huge coffee stain on the carpet at the front of the church, and I never again so much as even participated in another children's program.

Red Scooters

THE MOST MEMORABLE AND IMPORTANT Christmas Joe-brother and I ever had came on us by surprise. It was not the Christmas when we gave all my teachers toxic fruitcake cookies. Neither was it the year when Freddie Patton had tried to stop Joe-brother's basketball-induced nosebleed with his new bicycle pump. It was, instead, the year we learned all about Santa Claus.

I was ten years old, and Joe-brother was eight.

For the past couple of years, I had been hearing ugly rumors about the reality of Santa Claus. They were not to be taken seriously, because they seemed to be always whispered by those children whom any Santa Claus of justice would have given up on years before. Most of the no-necked Rabbit Creek kids came in this bunch, and I figured Santa Claus probably didn't even know where Rabbit Creek was.

This year, poor Joe-brother had begun to hear the same rumors. One day around Thanksgiving time he came home to say that as he was walking home from school, a car loaded with big kids had slowed down as they passed by. One of the big kids had stuck his head out the window and yelled, "There ain't no Santy Claus!" before the car sped away amid sounds of laughter.

Joe-brother told me about this with tears in his eyes, but neither one of us would dare tell Mother or Daddy.

The next time we saw Santa Claus we looked at one another but decided not to take any chances. We carefully told Santa what we wanted every time we saw him.

This year Joe-brother and I both wanted red scooters for Christmas—red scooters, metal with hard rubber wheels, the kind you put one foot on while you push with the other foot. (There was no pavement anywhere around our house so we never would know it was possible to actually get your speed up and coast with both feet off the ground.) The scooters we wanted had little brake levers you could step on that pushed against the rear wheel and skidded to a stop.

We showed Mother and Daddy the kind of scooters we wanted. Daddy just said, "They're awfully big."

Mostly, though, we told Santa Claus every chance we got. Mother would take us to town shopping on Saturdays. We'd go in the back door of Belk's Department Store and climb the stairs. At Belk's, the North Pole was on the second floor in the middle of Ladies' Ready-to-wear. There was cotton everywhere, and inside a little fence sat Santa Claus. I waited in line until it was finally my turn, and then I talked for both of us.

Joe-brother would not talk to Santa Claus for himself this year. Last year, on this very spot, Santa Claus had talked too long to Joe-brother, and in the end they were both wet. This year Joe-brother hid behind the ladies' woolen pants and waited for me to communicate for us both.

"What's your name, little boy?" Santa would say once I was firmly in his lap. "And what do you want for Christmas?"

I would tell him politely and also point out Joe-brother, who would be out of sight in the ladies' pants.

"We both want red scooters for Christmas," I would say. With an extra big "ho-ho-ho," Santa would put me down with two pieces of peppermint candy, one for me and one for Joe-brother.

Finished at Belk's, Mother would lead us across the street and into Harris's Department Store. Santa

Claus was fast! He was already there. We had just left him at Belk's not five minutes before, and here he was again! It also looked like he had had a difficult trip: his suit and beard were not quite as clean as they had been over at Belk's.

Joe-brother and I still weren't taking any chances. I got into line again while he hid in the shoe department and played with the shoehorns scattered there.

When I finally worked my way up to Santa Claus, I came to understand why it was important to talk to him several times. His memory was extremely bad. The first thing he said to me was, "What's your name, little boy? And what do you want for Christmas?"

I thought, *I just told you that—you tell me! Maybe you're getting too old for this job!* But what I did was tell him my name, very politely, and then point out Joe-brother and remind him again that he had us down for red scooters for Christmas.

Before the season was over, I had talked to Santa Claus while Joe-brother watched between twenty-five and thirty times. He never *once* remembered the scooters before I had to remind him.

The last day of school before Christmas was a Wednesday. We went to town to finish our shopping as soon as Mother got home from school. After shopping was done, we ended at Daddy's hardware store just after closing time. The four of us got in the Dodge and started home in the dark.

On the way home, we passed Jimmy's Drive-In Restaurant. Mother suggested, "Let's pick some food up at Jimmy's so I won't have to cook supper when we get home."

Daddy agreed, and we pulled into the curb-service side of the parking lot. Out came Jimmy himself to get our orders. Daddy ordered "four special cheeseburgers, four orders of fried potatoes, and four Co-colas."

In less than five minutes, Jimmy was coming back with the food. The cheeseburgers and potatoes were in a brown paper sack, and he carried the four unopened Cokes in one hand with the bottlenecks between his fingers. As he handed the order in the window and Daddy got his money out to pay, Jimmy said to Daddy, "You-all got any bottles to swap?" If we didn't have any empty Coke bottles, Daddy would have to pay a two-cent deposit on each bottle we took.

We always had empty bottles. I knew we did. There were always some in the trunk of the car. As I said, "I know where some bottles are," I was already out the car door and on my way back to the trunk.

You didn't need a key to open the trunk of the old blue Dodge—just turn the handle and lift. I did, and there before my eyes were two brand-new red scooters!

I slammed the trunk as fast as I could. "No bottles!" I said, as I climbed back into the car, flushed, looking only at the floor mat in the back-seat floor. Neither Daddy nor Mother said a word as we went home. We ate our supper quickly and went to bed.

Christmas morning finally came. Joe-brother got a wind-up toy train and I got a tool set from Santa Claus. We spent the whole morning playing and opening other presents.

A few of the cousins were with us for Christmas dinner, and we played together, compared and defended our several presents, until they all finally left in the middle of the afternoon.

Joe-brother and I were playing quietly when Daddy came into the living room. "How was Christmas?" he asked. "Did both of you get what you wanted?"

"Oh, yes!" we both insisted. "This is about the best Christmas we ever had! Santa Claus sure did a good job."

"Well, I'm glad," Daddy said. "Your mother and I were awful worried. You see, we knew you had been asking Santa Claus for scooters for Christmas. When we saw some scooters at the store, they were so big that we were just afraid that Santa Claus would never get down the chimney with them.

"So . . ." he was speaking softly now, almost a whispered secret, "your Mother and I got scooters for you for Christmas. We've had them hidden in the trunk of the car! You can go out there and get them now if you want to."

Later that night, Joe-brother and I talked. We still didn't know everything we wanted to know about Santa Claus. There would be more misadventures later. But we did decide that after this year it didn't matter what kids said at school or even what big kids yelled out of car windows, because, at best, the real Santa Claus only came around once a year anyway. We had found out a lot about our mother and daddy, and we had them all the time.

Slow Joe

AT HOME WE CALLED MY LITTLE brother "Joe-brother." When he started to school, all the teachers he had and the friends he made called him "Joe." That's because his name was "Joe." That was then, and this is now. If my brother, Joe, came in the door right this very minute, I would call him "Slow Joe."

It is a term of absolute respect. My brother, Joe, is the most patient person in the world. He never gets overly excited. He never gets upset. He never gets in a hurry. He is the most wonderfully calm and contented person I know.

When we were little boys, he was not like that. No, when we were little boys together, my little brother, Joe, could not wait! If he got hungry, he wanted food in his mouth at that very moment. If we were going to go somewhere, it was, "When are we going? . . . Why aren't we in the car?" Then, once we got in the car he started, "How much farther is it? . . . When are we going to get there?"

For a little kid like that, one of the most difficult times of the year is Christmas. When all of the presents from the gathering aunts and uncles began to accumulate under the tree at our house, he simply could not wait!

A daily holiday ritual began to develop around the time when he was four and I was six. Every day, when no one was paying any attention, he and I would wander into the living room. That's where the tree was put up and all the presents lived. We would go through every one of the presents, carefully examining the tags to try to read the names on them. We would shake every present, no matter whose name happened to be on it.

After that examination, we would pull out the presents that had our names on them (as well as we could tell), put them in two little piles, and count them to see who had the most. The piles then went way back behind the tree where no one could mess with them.

After that, we would walk out of the living room and I was finished with that for the day. Not my brother, Joe.

Some time later, when he was certain that no one was looking, he would sneak back into the living room and pull out one of his presents. He would hide behind a big wing chair in the living room, and, trying not to make a sound, he would open the present! He would not just open it a little bit to see what was in it. No, he would open it completely, take it out, and play with it. Then he was convinced that he could fix it back so that on one could tell that it had been opened!

The opened presents looked terrible. He couldn't even get things back into the box, the ribbon was gone, the paper was ripped. But he knew where our mother kept the tape! His self-deluded solution was to tape and tape and tape until all the loose ends were taped up, thus convincing himself—and the rest of the world, or so he thought—that the presents looked as perfect as when they had arrived at our house. By Christmas morning, every single present that had his name on it had been opened and played with quite a bit.

Now the big show came. We would all get up on Christmas morning, look briefly at what Santa Claus had brought, and head out to Grandma's house. I was dying to get to open some of my presents, but Joe-brother was vowing that he was in no hurry for his and he could easily wait until we got back.

Finally, late in the afternoon, we would return home from the big family celebration and tend to the presents we had left under the tree. Joe-brother would pick up one of his mangled, messy presents, hold it up in front of the family, and say: "Oh, I wonder what this is. It is from my Aunt Mary. I wonder what she got me?"

I would sit there and think, *You know exactly what it is . . . you've probably broken it already. Open it!*

Joe-brother would slowly open the present. (This was sometimes difficult through all of the tape he had added to cover his sins!) Then he would hold up a little toy, maybe a car or truck, and announce to the world: "Oh, look! I didn't know I was ever going to get something like this!"

Everyone would laugh. I would sit there, disgusted at the whole thing, thinking to myself, *Yeah . . . and you're a big, fat liar! That's what you are!*

We got older. I was about nine years old and Joe-brother was about seven. There were still lots of things to be figured out about Christmas, but one thing was sure. Joe-brother would never make it to Christmas morning with a present that hadn't already been opened.

It was about a week before school was scheduled to get out for Christmas when Joe-brother came home in a terrible mood. He was fussing and growling all over the place.

"What's the matter with you today?" Mother asked.

"Something *terrible* happened at school today," was his vague reply.

"What was it?" Mother pursued.

"Something *terrible!*" he vowed.

"Well," she insisted, "what?"

"*Terrible!*" was all he could bring himself to say.

Finally Joe-brother talked about the terrible day. It seemed that, at school, some kids he called "those old bad boys" had told him that if you were personally bad, Santa Claus wouldn't bring you anything good for Christmas. But you couldn't let yourself think he had just forgotten you. Oh, no! If you were bad, they had told him, Santa Claus would bring you lots of lumps of coal and enough switches so you could get punished all year without anybody even having to go get a switch. They would be right there!

We all listened to the "terrible" report, then Mother asked. "What's the trouble? Have you been bad?"

"*Nooo!*" Joe-brother insisted, but the speed of his denial gave everything away.

Mother began to try to unravel the problem. "Listen," she started out. "Santa Claus is good. Santa Claus would never bring you coal and switches. You don't have to worry about Santa Claus!"

The reassurance must have overdone it, because

in the next breath, Joe-brother's normal smart mouth was back.

"I'm not afraid of Santa Claus, anyway!" he now avowed.

Mother seemed to have an interest in just where this was going, so she led him on with enough rope for him to finish his line of thought.

"And what do you mean by that?" was her first question.

"Santa Claus doesn't know anything!" was his declaration.

"And what do you mean by that?" the question was the same.

"Every time you see him, you have to tell him your name! He can't tell one little kid from another one!" His mouth was running now, and he just couldn't seem to get the lid back on it! "One time Santa Claus asked me if I had been bad. If he doesn't know, I'm not going to tell him! . . . I'm not scared of Santa Claus!"

I heard all of that. Mother heard all of that. Daddy, who always loved to think up new tricks, heard all of that. I could see in the corner of his eyes the little grinning wrinkles that always seemed to mean TROUBLE!

That year, as usual, Joe-brother opened every one of his Christmas presents before Christmas.

Christmas morning came, and he and I rushed down to the living room to see what had happened since bedtime. There in the living room, unwrapped and ready for play as always, were the presents Santa Claus had brought both of us. I proceeded to survey and then try out the first of my presents, a metal-boxed Erector Set. Joe-brother just stood there, looking around at the toys in the room.

Just then Mother and Daddy came into the living room. Mother saw me playing, then looked at Joe-brother. "Why don't you see what Santa Claus brought you before we go to Grandmother's?" she asked him.

"I told you," he answered, which made no sense to anyone.

"You told us what?" Mother went on.

"I told you," he now insisted, "that Santa Claus didn't know anything."

"What are you talking about? He brought you some nice toys," Mother insisted.

"That's exactly what I am talking about." Now it was Joe-brother's turn. "See . . . Santa Claus brought me good stuff . . . and *I've been baaad!!!*" He laughed out loud.

I couldn't believe this was going on. Mother didn't say anything. Daddy's eyes twinkled. Then he suggested, "Well, why don't we go ahead now and open the presents from the family? Joe, you go first."

My brother Joe picked up his first present. He held it up, turned it over and over in his hands, and looked at it. Anyone could tell that it had been totally opened and then rewrapped.

"Oh," he started. "I wonder what this is? It's from my Aunt Esther. Oh, I wonder what she brought me?"

Get on with it, I thought. *Open it. If every present takes this long, this is going to take a hundred years.*

Slowly Joe-brother opened the messy package. He carefully pulled out the paper inside, and when he looked down into the box, there was a rock in it!

"Well," Daddy asked, "what did you get?"

Joe-brother barely whispered so that no one could really hear him. "A rock."

"What did you say?" Daddy smiled at his own overly innocent inquiry.

"A rock!!! Can't you hear anything?" Joe-brother fairly screamed. Then he repeated over and over again, "A rock . . . a rock . . . a rock."

Try another one," Daddy offered. "This one's from Uncle Spencer. Let's see what he got for you. He'll be out there at Grandmother's and you can tell him what you think about it."

Joe-brother picked up the long box that was being handed to him and slowly opened it. Inside, carefully nested in white tissue paper, was a bundle of switches with red ribbons tied around them.

Still Joe-brother didn't give up. He kept opening presents. Pretty soon he found lumps of coal. He also got some empty dog food cans that had not even been washed out and had rotten, stinking dog food juice dripping out of them. He got broken glass, a rotten banana, and even an Electrolux vacuum cleaner bag that was already used and full of dust and dirt! By the time he had finished all of his openings, there was a big pile of pure trash on the living room floor, but not one single toy!

Daddy was smiling as he asked, "I wonder why that happened?"

"I don't know," was Joe-brother's shrugged answer.

Mother now tried. "I thought you said that Santa Claus doesn't know anything. What do you think now?"

By now, Joe-brother was crying. "Santa Claus doesn't know anything . . . see . . . he brought me good stuff even if I had been bad. He really doesn't know anything. All of this old terrible mess . . . it all came from our own family!!!"

"Maybe," Daddy suggested, "maybe your own family knows more than Santa Claus."

Then Daddy walked into his and Mother's

bedroom. When he came back out, all of the toys Joe-brother had already opened were in his arms.

"Oh," Joe-brother said with recognition. *"You did it!"*

Later on in the day, when someone at Grandmother's asked him what he got for Christmas, he simply ran into the bedroom and slammed the door without even answering the question.

The next year it was about a week before Christmas when Mother came home from school with an idea. "I know that it is so hard to wait," she acknowledged. "I have an idea. What if we each pick out one present to open before Christmas?"

Joe-brother was out with an immediate answer. "That's *not* a good idea," he insisted. "That might ruin everything!"

After that year, no presents were ever opened early again, and that's the year that Joe-brother started to become the most patient person in the whole world!

"Don't Kill Santa!"

THE LITTLE HOUSE ON PLOTT CREEK WAS built around an almost central chimney. At one time there had been four fireplaces, one for each room except for the kitchen, which had its own chimney that connected to the wood cookstove. Through the years, the bedroom fireplaces had been closed up and plastered over so that, in my childhood, only the living-room fireplace remained in use.

That was enough for Santa Claus! We were born already knowing that Santa Claus came down the chimney. Before bedtime, we let our stockings hang visibly from the mantle and left cookies and milk beside the fireplace so he would be especially generous with us. Keeping Santa happy was a big deal.

Our family always had a big Christmas tree in the living room at Plott Creek. At my grandmother's house, the Christmas tree was cut somewhere on the farm and brought to the house, but since we lived in town, we proudly bought our tree on the corner lot where they were sold by the Lion's Club.

There was a good reason for this Christmas tree to be big. Mama had six sisters and, except for only one who lived nearby, they all had married and moved far away. When the relatives came home for Christmas, with an increasing number of cousins every year, our house was one of the major sleeping places, Grandmother's being the other one.

After all, we had a chimney and an open fireplace. So, it was safe for the cousins to write or talk to Santa Claus and let him know to bring their stuff to our house. Long before Christmas day our tree was surrounded by piles of presents to, from, and between all of the cousins. The very air was full of talk about what we knew would be coming down our shared chimney.

I loved checking out all of the presents under the tree to see for whom they were intended. Of course, the real reason for such curious close examination was to check on which presents were intended for me and to guess their contents.

With so many relatives about, we got lots of presents. But Joe-brother and I never received wrapped presents under the tree from Mama and Daddy. We never had gotten presents this way, and we simply accepted this to be normal. I figured that, first of all, we got everything that we needed from Santa Claus, and with all the relatives visiting and eating all of our food, Mama and Daddy didn't have enough extra money to buy more stuff for us. (We did, however, from our weekly allowances, always manage to get presents for them.)

So all the world was normal, and Santa Claus came down the chimney the way we knew that he always had and always would.

Then we got the oil heater.

It was in the summertime after I was in the second grade. There must have been a summertime sale on at Massie's Furniture Company. Daddy came home early from the bank to meet the truck when it arrived at our house with the big purchase he had made. It was a two-tone enamel-finished brown and tan Siegler oil space heater.

Daddy both helped and directed the two men from the furniture store as they went about their delivery business. They sealed up the fireplace with a heavy sheet of metal that covered up the opening and itself had a special round hole just big enough for the stovepipe from the oil heater. Then they maneuvered the beautiful brown and tan stove into place on the living-room hearth and slid the short length of stovepipe into its proper place.

One of the men took a brace and bit and bored a

hole through the baseboard nearest to the back of the stove. As I watched, the other man, who had crawled under the house, pushed a length of copper tubing up through the hole.

The inside end of the long copper tube was attached to the new oil heater. When I went outside to see what was happening out there, the other end was being attached to what looked like a sideways barrel on legs that had been put up against the house right outside Mama and Daddy's bedroom window. "This is the oil tank," the men told Daddy. "They'll come from Reed's tomorrow and fill it up with number two. It'll hold fifty-five gallons and that will last you for a while . . . if you don't run it all the time."

When the first cold weather came in October, we discovered what a miracle the Siegler oil heater turned out to be. Daddy would turn a knob on the back of the heater, then open a little door on the front. He would watch the inside of the firebox until he could see a little bit of heating oil coming in. Then he would light a Kleenex with a match and toss the burning Kleenex into the firebox. The oil would catch fire, he would close the little door on the stove, and it would start to heat up.

The oil heater even had a three-speed fan built right into the bottom of it. After it got heated up, you could turn on the fan and hot air would blow out. "My feet will never be cold again!" Mama declared with joy as she pulled up a little rocking chair and put her feet right in front of the fan duct.

Everything was fine through the cool nights of late October. All was well through the gradually colder days of November. Then, with the coming of December, all of our warm joy suddenly came to an end. Thanksgiving had come and gone and the stores in town started slowly decorating for Christmas. One day we came home from doing some shopping in town. When we came in the door, Joe-brother, now about six years old, burst into tears.

Mama ran to him. "Are you hurt? Are you hurt? What in the world is wrong?"

"Look!" Joe-brother pointed. "We got that new oil stove and now we don't have a fireplace for Santa Claus to come through! He'll try to come down the chimney the way he always does and he'll get sucked into that oil heater and he'll burn all up and it will be our fault and everyone in the world will know!"

"What will be our fault?" Mama looked fascinated and mystified at the same time.

"We're going to kill Santa Claus and nobody in the world will ever get any more Christmas presents! It will be all our fault!"

Mama didn't even try to figure this out. She waited for Daddy to get home. Somehow she knew that this was in his department, and somehow we all knew that he would figure this out.

Joe met Daddy at the door when he got home from work. He laid out the problem, whimpering between halting words. Daddy just stood in the living room and listened, then he looked at the stove like he was studying it for a while. He looked as if he were trying to determine whether somehow Santa Claus could still squeeze in that way. He opened the little door on the front of the heater and peered into the firebox. He shook his head.

"This is going to take some real thought, boys. You'd better give me until Saturday to think about it." He turned to Mama and said, "We may just have to take out the heater and freeze again!"

She shook her head and softly said, half to herself, "Joe, Joe, Joe . . ."

Saturday came, and right after breakfast Daddy told us he had it all worked out. He got us to put on our coats to keep warm, and then we went with him out to the wooden garage in the back yard.

Daddy hunted around until he found a couple of scraps of plywood about two feet square. Then he poked along the side of the garage among the half-used paint cans until he found some red and some green enamel. "We can't use white paint, boys. In case it snows for Christmas, white wouldn't show up."

We helped carry the wood scraps and the paint back to the kitchen, where Mama fussed while Daddy covered the kitchen table with layers of newspaper.

First we painted the scraps of plywood bright red. "We'd better use Christmas colors," he said, "so Santa Claus will know that we're talking to him." Joe and I still had no idea what we were doing or what Daddy had in mind.

It took most of the day for the red paint to dry, even in the hot kitchen. Mama kept fussing around about "when all this mess and bad smell are out of the kitchen." By late afternoon the red paint had all dried until you could touch it without it sticking to your fingers anymore.

"Now the hard part starts," Daddy announced. With a pencil he carefully outlined the words we were now to paint in green onto the red sign boards. One was to say: CHIMNEY CLOSED! DO NOT ENTER! USE THE FRONT DOOR! Two big green arrows pointed down. As we carefully filled out his pencilled letters with small brushes, Daddy described how we would wire the sign to the chimney so that Santa Claus would be absolutely sure to see it when he landed on the roof.

The second sign was to go on the front of the house beside the front door. ENTER HERE! it said. THE DOOR IS NOT LOCKED! Two arrows pointed toward the door just in case Santa Claus didn't spot it immediately. Even in those safe old days it was a miracle that the house wasn't robbed with that sign hanging on the front door for two weeks before Christmas!

We waited until Sunday afternoon, after church and after dinner, to put up the new signs. By now they had dried overnight and the enamel was completely hardened.

Joe-brother and I put on our old clothes to help, but we had to stand on the ground and watch while Daddy climbed up the ladder he had just leaned up to the roof over the front porch of the house. He carried the CHIMNEY CLOSED sign and several pieces of coat-hanger wire. He wired the sign to the chimney where not only Santa Claus but any one who drove up or down Plott Creek Road could clearly read it.

Joe-brother and I got to help hang the ENTER HERE sign on a nail Daddy drove into the house on the right side of the front door.

Now all was well. When Christmas came, Santa Claus saw the sign on the chimney and came in through the front door the way he now knew he was supposed to. We knew this because both our presents and the presents for the visiting cousins were safely placed around the oil heater on Christmas morning.

When I was twelve years old we moved. This move was pivotal in many ways for our family. We only went three miles, yet it was like moving from one country to another.

The new house was different in every possible way: it had a paved driveway and it had central heat. It had wall-to-wall carpeting and a big fireplace in the living room. Since we moved in the summertime, we had no initial interest in or even notice of the fireplace. That would come later.

The new house had a big, bayed-out picture window in the front of the living room. When December came, we all decided that the picture-window recess was the perfect place for our Christmas tree. This year's tree was bigger than ever. It was a good thing, too, because a continually growing number of cousins meant that we needed all the space we could get for the bigger-than-ever accumulation of family presents.

It was the same day that we put up the Christmas tree that we realized how important the new fireplace was. At this new house, Santa Claus would not have to come in through the front door! Now he could go back to coming down the chimney the way we knew he liked to come in, the way he ought to come in, the way he was supposed to come in.

It was Joe who spoke up. "We won't have to put the sign on the chimney over here at this house. Our chimney is open for business again!"

Mama and Daddy heard all this, and Mama said, "Yes, boys, you are older now and there are some things that little boys do that you have about out-grown." This reply from her did not make any sense in the world to either Joe or to me. I thought, *We didn't outgrow anything, we just got a proper house with a fireplace again.*

When school got out for Christmas, all the rela-tives started to come in for the holidays. As they arrived, the collection of presents under our Christmas tree proceeded to grow. Daily, Joe and I would exam-ine the labels to see who all of the presents were for and especially to see whether there was anything new for either of us.

It was about a week before Christmas now, and Joe and I were checking the presents once again. All of a sudden he almost yelled, "Look at this!" He was examining two big presents we had not seen before now. They were different from one another, but both of them were long and heavy. And . . . they were for us, from Mama and Daddy.

This had never happened before. The two of us got so much from Santa Claus and from everyone else that there had never been wrapped presents under the tree from our parents. "We must have gotten rich!" I cried. "First a new house, and now Christmas presents from Mama and Daddy . . . all in the same year!" Neither of us could believe it!

Joe and I took turns handling and shaking the big presents. They were both heavy but slightly different from one another. We hadn't even asked for anything from our parents, so we couldn't imagine what they might be. We would just have to wait.

Finally it was Christmas Eve. At supper we sat around the table looking forward to all that was coming on the next day. Everyone in Mama's family was coming to our house for dinner since the new house was bigger than Grandma's. The pile of presents under the tree was huge, and there would be a great one-at-a-time opening ceremony later on in the day.

I offered my twelve-year-old wisdom: "I've said it before and I'll say it again, there's one thing that we don't need at this new house—that old sign that we used to put up on the chimney on Plott Creek."

"Yes," Mama agreed. "Some things get a lot easier as you boys get older."

I still didn't get it. *What does getting older have to*

do with anything? I thought. *We have a fireplace here, and that it all there is to it.*

We never ever fussed about going to bed. The earlier we went to bed, the earlier we would be up the next day. It was no later than eight-thirty when Joe and I headed off to our room to spend our first Christmas Eve in the new house.

Having neither watches ourselves nor a clock in the bedroom, we had no idea what time it was when we awakened. It was Joe who woke up, and he called over to me in my bed. "Is it time to get up?"

"We're awake, aren't we? I don't know what time it is, but it has to be after midnight . . . so . . . it's morning!" Still I wanted him to go in front into the living room just in case we stumbled onto Santa Claus while he was still there. I followed in the dark while he led the way down the hall toward the dim glow of the Christmas tree lights that we had left plugged in all night.

My brother stopped still in the doorway to the living room like he was frozen in place. I could not see past him into the dimly lit space to see what he was staring at so intensely. Suddenly, Joe screamed and fell to the floor crying.

Then I could see it all. He had been staring at nothing! Santa Claus had not come! Except for the wrapped gifts under the tree, there was nothing more than the ordinary furnishings in the living room.

"Santa Claus didn't come! Santa Claus didn't come!" he wailed over and over again. Tears filled my eyes as I arrived at the same awful reality. What had we done that was so very bad to have caused this disaster?

Suddenly Mama and Daddy burst into the living room. They had been awakened by my brother's screaming cries. "What in the world is going on in here?" Mama asked. "Stop crying so we can figure out what is wrong!"

Joe-brother and I both quieted down to a whimper. I tried to explain, "We got up to see what we got . . . and . . . and we didn't get anything! Santa Claus didn't even come! What did we do that was bad enough for this?"

When I looked at my mama for an answer, she was not looking at me. Instead she was looking at Daddy with a horror-stricken expression on her face. She spoke quietly and directly to him. "Oh, Joe . . . I thought they were old enough to know . . ."

Daddy interrupted her, but he was speaking firmly and directly to the two of us. "What your mama means, boys, is that she thought you two were old enough to know not to get up this early. Don't you know that

Santa Claus comes to see the smallest kids first in case they accidently wake up? He gets around to boys your age last, because he knows that you are supposed to stay in the bed until it is daylight. Now you go back to bed, quick. I think you got here just before he did. Santa Claus hasn't been here . . . yet!"

Joe-brother and I headed back to bed, wiping our eyes all the way. We did go back to sleep, and we slept quite a long time. Even when we woke up, we were in no hurry at all to get out of bed and go back into the living room. It was scary to think that Daddy may have been wrong. Maybe Santa Claus meant to miss our house on purpose!

Late in the morning, way after daylight, Mama came to the bedroom door and called to us. "Boys . . . you'd better get up! Breakfast is ready, and . . . you'd better come and see what Santa Claus brought you!"

I could not keep up with Joe-brother. He was making a full-speed break for the living room. When we got there, sure enough, Santa Claus had come. There was an Erector Set with Joe's name on it and a big chemistry set for me. "Just what we both have been talking about!" I offered. Even before we could eat the hotcakes Mama had waiting for us, we had to open the boxes and look at all of the parts and pieces.

All morning Joe-brother built things and I did

chemistry experiments. We never even started to open the under-the-tree presents until all of the rest of the relatives got there and finished Christmas dinner.

Finally, dinner was over and the dishes were all washed. All of the family—Daddy and Mama, Joe, Grandma and Granddaddy, the aunts and uncles and all the cousins—gathered in the living room and the great gift opening started.

It took all afternoon; after all, only one present could be opened at a time. The smallest cousins got to crawl around under the tree and take out one gift at a time. They would bring it to a grownup who could read, the name would be announced, and the gift would be opened.

As the afternoon passed, we all gradually accumulated our own little hordes of presents. All was well and wonderful.

At the time, I did not see anything at all out of order. Later, however, Joe-brother and I were playing in the garage with his new Erector Set when I noticed some wadded-up wrapping paper stuck in a grocery bag beside the garage door, like someone had intended to carry it out but did not get all the way there. *Who opened their presents out here?* I wondered. *I thought we opened all of them in the house.*

Then another realization hit me. When we had

opened the "under-the-tree" presents, there had been no wrapped gifts there for Joe-brother and me from Mama and Daddy. But the day was too good to ask pointless questions, so we just built with the Erector Set and mixed chemicals to see what would happen and tried not to think too critically about anything or anyone.

It was the following December when, on a Saturday, Daddy gathered the two of us after breakfast and said, "Come on, boys, we need to do something to start getting the house ready for Christmas."

"Are we going to get our Christmas tree already?" Joe-brother asked.

"No," Daddy replied. "It's something even more important than a Christmas tree."

We followed him out to the laundry room behind the new garage and watched as he rummaged in the shelves to find red and green paint. We followed him to the trunk of the Plymouth as he opened it and pulled out two new pieces of plywood, each one about eighteen inches square. We followed him back into the new kitchen where we watched him spread newspaper all over the kitchen table. And we listened while Mama said, "Not again, Joe."

Joe-brother and I painted the boards green and left them, with their strong oil-paint smell, to dry in the kitchen. That night, when the green was dry, we followed Daddy's guidance as he outlined and directed the painting of two new signs.

Chimney Open! the first one said. Come on Down! The other sign said, Door Locked . . . Try the Chimney.

When everything was dry on Sunday afternoon, after church and after Sunday dinner, Joe-brother and I changed out of our Sunday clothes and helped Daddy hang the signs. We were big enough now to climb the ladder with him and go right up on the roof where we wired the first sign firmly to the chimney. And we were big enough to drive our own nail in the side of the house to hang the second sign beside the front door.

"Santa Claus has a big job, boys," Daddy said. "He has to go to a lot of houses. It's easy for him to get confused. It's best to try to help him out all that we can. I don't think he'll make any more mistakes like he did last year."

And . . . he never did!

The Last Time
It Snowed

WE LIVED AT THE OLD HOUSE ON PLOTT
Creek from the time I was born until we moved at the
end of the year when I was in the sixth grade. After
that we lived in the "new house." When that house
was sold forty-three years later, after Mama's death,
Joe-brother and I still called it "the new house."

There are more Christmas memories that cluster
around the old house than the new one, partly because
we lived there twice as many of my growing-up years.
But one Christmas at the new house still lives forever.

At the old house on Plott Creek, the only neighbors within shouting distance were all old. There
were no children at all, and Joe-brother and I were
reduced to that miserable state of having to actually
play with one another.

But when we moved to the new house, we were

back-yard-to-back-yard neighbors with the Leather-woods. It was absolutely wonderful. I was twelve years old, and Larry Leatherwood was almost the same age. My little brother, Joe, was ten years old, and Larry's little brother, Ronnie, was ten years old. There we were, four boys, separated from one another only by the fence between the two back yards. The four of us played together after school in the school year, on weekends all year, and for days on end in the summer. School holidays were especially exciting times, for there were always extra activities to go along with the play.

The only problem with the entire arrangement was the fence between the two back yards. Whenever we did something we had either already been told not to do—or anything that the basic moral code of the universe told us not to do without our even having to hear it from a parent—that fence came into play.

"Meet me at the fence" were words we were loathe to hear from any of our parents. The fence was the place of 1950s pre-ego-sensitive cruel-but-not-unusual punishment.

A little sassafras tree grew by that back-yard fence, and when *"Meet me at the fence"* came down as the sentence, any of the four us us, or some combination of the four, was about to get a "little dose of sassafras tea."

Sassafras tea came in the form of a green limb switching on either your bottom or your legs that was guaranteed to produce good behavior for at least half-a-day following it! We were then always told that when we were old enough to act grown up, we would no longer need sassafras tea but could work things out "more reasonably." How we all looked forward to that day.

Larry and I seemed to be called to the fence more than either (or both) of our little brothers. The reason for that may have been that Larry and I loved science experiments, and we usually performed the experiments on one or both of the little brothers. This was actually more fun and more educational than having chemistry sets to begin with.

The Christmas after we moved next door to the Leatherwoods was the first white Christmas in my childhood memory. On top of that, it was the year Joe-brother and I got our first sleds since here we had hills that we had not had near the old house.

The sledding hill was the cow pasture beside the Leatherwoods' house. It was a long open hill that ran down and down and then had a slight upturn to help you stop before you headed back to the top for the next great slide. On the entire hillside there was only one small tree: an apple tree that stood nearly in the center of the slope and was totally easy to avoid as you slid past it.

We took dozens of trips on the new Flexible Flyers. Then one of the little boys had to go to the bathroom. They both headed to the Leatherwoods' house while Larry and I continued to accumulate more trips down the hill.

Suddenly it came to us like a gift from God: an idea! We didn't think it up, we didn't plan it out. It was a gift that came into both our heads so freely that we couldn't help but act upon it. Larry and I headed up to the top of the hill with the longest of the Flexible Flyers. I sat on the sled while he held on to the rope and let me slowly glide down the hillside. We headed straight toward the apple tree.

Once the sled got right up to the apple tree, I slipped off the side and stood up. Then we got down to business. Larry and I tilted the sled up onto one runner and let it make a single runner track down beside one side of the apple tree. Then we took the sled back above the tree, tilted it the other way, and made an identical track down beside the opposite side of the tree.

After that, Larry and I placed the sled carefully in the tracks below the tree where we both got on the sled and waited. Just as the little boys came back around the corner from their trip to the bathroom,

Larry and I pushed off on the sled and went sliding down the hill, laughing and screaming all the way.

"Oh, that was fun!" I yelled.

Larry continued, "Oh, it tickled, it tickled! Ha, ha, ha!"

Joe-brother and Ronnie came running. "What did you do?" they wanted to know. "What was so much fun?"

Without any practice or collusion in the world, Larry and I answered together, "We slid through the tree! Oh, did it tickle!"

"No, you didn't," they both insisted.

"Oh yes we did . . . just look at our tracks!" The two of them stared, not with logical disbelief but with a kind of suspension of good sense that told us instantly we had been successful.

Larry and I didn't even suggest it. We simply stood there and watched as Joe-brother and Ronnie pulled the big sled up to the top of the hill so they could personally find out how much fun it was to actually slide through the apple tree. They got on the sled in a sort of double-deck way, belly down, with one on the back of the other. So, as they came down the hill, gaining speed all the way, they were coming headfirst toward the apple tree.

It would not have changed what happened to them, but it might have changed what happened to us, if Larry and I had been able to simply stand there and watch quietly. But at the last moment, when it was too late to act but not too late to yell, we had a horrible attack of conscience. "Stop! It won't work!" we both yelled, just as we saw the little boys score a direct hit on the apple tree.

They got up, dazed, each with a growing knot at the same place on his forehead and now possessing the sure and deadly knowledge that Larry and I were to blame for their personal pain and suffering.

As it turned out, we didn't get in trouble. At the time we thought that they had withheld telling on us so that our parents wouldn't know how stupid they had been again. Later we figured out that sometimes punishment credits are stored until there are enough to make a more significant withdrawal.

The snow melted after Christmas. We went back to school, now looking forward to spring while at the same time hoping that next year might bring another white Christmas.

Both families had television sets by now. We loved television, even though we got only one black and white channel. Every Sunday night our families, or at least the boys, seemed to end up at one house or the other to watch television. The best shows were on Sunday night.

One Sunday night we were watching a special

show from the *Wonderful World of Disney.* It was all about the life of Davy Crockett. Davy Crockett and his cohorts were out in the woods somewhere, and they were digging a pit to serve as a trap to catch an animal for food.

Daddy kept talking all the way through the program. "We used to do that when I was a boy on the farm"—he couldn't keep from telling us how everything in the world reminded him of his own childhood. "All you have to do is to dig the hole deep enough so that whatever you catch can't jump out. If it's a bear it better be deep, because if it gets out it will be so mad it just might kill you."

He kept talking. It seemed that Daddy knew more about trapping animals than Davy Crockett—or was it Fess Parker he was correcting?—had ever known. "After you dig the hole, you put some bait in it that will make the animal come to it. Then you cover it over with little thin sticks and limbs and stuff. Then they fall right in."

After the show was over, Larry and I were talking. Suddenly another free idea came to us: "That animal-trap trick will work with little brothers!" a voice seemed to say. And the plan was made.

As soon as we could spend significant time out of doors in the springtime, Larry and I started on the "Great Little Brother Trap." We picked a place that was down in the woods on the opposite side of the hill from the sledding pasture, a spot that was well away from the house, hidden in trees where no parents were likely to wander accidently. We marked off the place, and the digging started.

Since both of our fathers had big gardens in the back yards between the two houses, Larry and I decided that the best way to hide what we were doing was to carry each bucketload of dirt up the hill and scatter it around in one of the gardens. It was a lot of work, but this plan assured that, once we covered the hole, there would be no piles of dirt nearby to give away its existence.

It was very important for the hole to be deep enough. We knew that once we caught Joe-brother and Ronnie, they would really kill us if they could get back out. We dug the hole so deep that we had to drag a stepladder down from the garage to both finish the hole and get ourselves back out. We decided that it was indeed as deep as it needed to be. (The one thing we didn't think about was what we were actually going to *do* to our captives once we got them.)

After the hole was finished, we carefully created a network of small pine branches to cover it, filling it over with grass and leaves until you could not tell at all that the pit was there. It was a perfect little brother trap!

The problem now was to find a way to bait them to fall in.

Spring had come through the weeks of digging the hole. Every day we invited Joe-brother and Ronnie to play in the woods, but no matter what we tried, they simply would not be tricked into running across the covered hole.

Easter weekend arrived. Part of the weekend's events included a big Easter egg hunt involving both families. Larry and I actually put a visible egg right out on top of the trap hole. Joe-brother and Ronnie hunted eggs all afternoon and never did see that one.

At one point during the Easter egg hunt, Daddy and Mr. Leatherwood stumbled upon a new spring-time yellow jacket's nest in the woods. They saw the yellow jackets and warned us away before anyone got stung. Daddy said, "As soon as the sun goes down, I will take care of those little gentlemen!"

As the day went on, all the boys forgot about the yellow jackets.

Late in the day, just after sunset, we were playing in the yard when we all saw smoke coming up out of the woods. Joe-brother and Ronnie led the race to see what was making the smoke. When we got there, we discovered that Daddy and Mr. Leatherwood had poured kerosene on the yellow jackets' nest and were burning out the bees.

That's where we got the idea. Smoke! That made everyone run to see what caused it. If we could just make smoke come up out of the trap hole, Joe-brother and Ronnie would certainly run toward it in curiosity and we would have them! The plan was made.

The next day was Easter Monday, a school and work holiday. Both families were at home. Time to strike!

Larry and I took a big bunch of newspaper from the back of the garage to the trap. We pushed many wads of newspaper down through the camouflage of the hole. Then we squirted charcoal lighter fluid down on the newspaper and dropped a match on the whole mess.

Larry and I hid behind thick locust and honeysuckle brush as we looked up toward the back yards awaiting the arrival of our little brothers. The smoke was pouring up through the leaves and grass over the trap hole, and we knew they would soon be on the way.

There were two things that Larry and I did not realize. The first was that Joe-brother and Ronnie were not even playing outside; they were inside our house watching television. The other thing we had no awareness of was that since both of our fathers were home from work on this holiday, they were working nearly side by side in their two gardens in the back yards on top of the hill.

As Larry and I were watching for our little brothers, our fathers were having a conversation. One of them said something like, "Look down toward the woods! There's smoke coming from something!" Suddenly we saw the two of them come to the edge of the hill, looking toward the smoke. I heard Mr. Leatherwood say to my daddy, "There's a fire in the woods, Joe! Let's run and stomp it out!"

Down the hill Larry and I watched the Vice-president of the bank and the Superintendent of Schools running, their garden hoes carried like weapons, headed toward the smoking trap hole.

Now if Larry and I had simply stayed quiet and hidden, they might never have known who dug the hole or why it was there. They might later have even thought Martians had invaded the hillside and planned the whole thing!

But, instead of staying quietly hidden, Larry and I had another terrible attack of conscience. At the exact moment when it was too late to stop them, we jumped out of hiding and yelled, *"Nooo! It's not for you!"* At that very moment two middle-aged men disappeared into the ground.

We listened to them flail around for a few moments, making sure that the fire was out before they started yelling for us. As they began to yell for us, we realized that we had indeed dug the hole deep enough, because without help, there was no possible way they could get out!

Without ever saying it to one another, for a few moments there Larry and I were both assessing the wisdom of packing our bags and leaving town.

Suddenly it seemed like the only sounds we could hear in the world were both of our fathers angrily calling us with tones of voice that, in themselves, almost pulled us toward them. "You two come over here . . . get us out of here! Go get a stepladder right now! You're going to be in big trouble for this!!"

We walked slowly up to the hole out of which came lingering smoke, dust, and thick language! Larry and I looked down to see both of our fathers hopelessly trapped in the hole intended for deserving little brothers. Our fathers were flailing around and trying their best to sustain all of their anger. Without help, they would never get out.

When Larry realized that these two grown men were dependent upon us for their rescue, he got the idea that perhaps he had some bargaining power. He looked down into the hole and, with all the bravado of a desperate thirteen-year-old, said, "We'll make a deal with you!"

That did it! The two fathers could no longer maintain their anger. They broke out into laughter, and soon all four of us stood there laughing our heads off for four or five minutes. This was great!

Finally Mr. Leatherwood said, "What's the deal?"

I decided to let Larry do all the talking since this was all his idea from the start. "We'll get you out of the hole," he bargained, "if you won't take us to the fence and give us sassafras tea!"

Both fathers laughed. Then one of them said, "You're too old for that! We already told you that. You're not going to get a spanking. We'll think up something else for you."

That suited Larry, even though I was suspicious of the whole thing. He figured that nothing could be as bad as a spanking.

We both walked up the hill to the garage behind our house, got the same stepladder we had used to build the hole to begin with, and dragged it back down the hill to our waiting prisoners. We slid the ladder down into the hole, and in no time, the fathers were out!

"Now," we both said, "what are you going to do to us? We saved you, remember."

It was my father who spoke for the both of them this time. "We've already started to think about that," he said. "While you were going to get the ladder we both decided that the first thing you are going to have to do is to fill up this hole."

That didn't seem like such a hard thing when

they said it. But, as we later discovered, with the gardens now growing full and thick, by the time we scratched out each bucketful of dirt from between the rows and carried them one at a time to the big hole, it would be late summer!

That was not, however, the end of the punishment. "There's more." They were taking turns talking now, like two cops threatening a criminal on *Dragnet*.

"What is it?" we wanted to know.

"We've decided that the fairest punishment of all would be, if we have another white Christmas, we all want to come out and watch while the two of you teach the little boys how to ride the sled through the apple tree! That's a fit punishment for boys your age!"

"You know what?" Larry sounded like he was bargaining again now. "I don't actually think we are too old to get a spanking. I'd be pretty sure it's going to snow again this year. So I think instead you ought to give us a dose of sassafras tea!"

So in the end, we all marched to the fence between the yards for the last time. Both fathers ritually broke limbs off the sassafras tree, Larry and I leaned over the fence, and we all four laughed again as the world's weakest dose of tea was offered. It was our last spanking ever.

And as far as I can remember, we never ever had a white Christmas again!